Could Nancy be a

"What's wrong?" Nancy asked as she entered the living room. Mrs. Rutledge was pacing back and forth and holding Baby. The twins were sitting side by side on the sofa. Olivia stood in the back near the fireplace.

"On Monday afternoon when the twins went to play with the dollhouse," Mrs. Rutledge announced, "they noticed that five pieces of furniture were missing."

Missing? Nancy stared at Mrs. Rutledge. "That's awful!" she gasped.

Nancy's mind started to race. *Does Mrs. Rutledge know I am a detective? Does she want me to find the missing furniture?* Before she could ask, Veronica pointed her finger at Nancy.

"She did it, Grandma! *Nancy* stole the dollhouse furniture!"

The Nancy Drew Notebooks

# 1 The Slumber Party Secret	#30 It's No Joke!
# 2 The Lost Locket	#31 The Fine-Feathered Mystery
# 3 The Secret Santa	#32 The Black Velvet Mystery
# 4 Bad Day for Ballet	#33 The Gumdrop Ghost
# 5 The Soccer Shoe Clue	#34 Trash or Treasure?
# 6 The Ice Cream Scoop	#35 Third-Grade Reporter
# 7 Trouble at Camp Treehouse	#36 The Make-Believe Mystery
# 8 The Best Detective	#37 Dude Ranch Detective
# 9 The Thanksgiving Surprise	#38 Candy Is Dandy
#10 Not Nice on Ice	#39 The Chinese New Year Mystery
#11 The Pen Pal Puzzle	#40 Dinosaur Alert!
#12 The Puppy Problem	#41 Flower Power
#13 The Wedding Gift Goof	#42 Circus Act
#14 The Funny Face Fight	#43 The Walkie-talkie Mystery
#15 The Crazy Key Clue	#44 The Purple Fingerprint
#16 The Ski Slope Mystery	#45 The Dashing Dog Mystery
#17 Whose Pet Is Best?	#46 The Snow Queen's Surprise
#18 The Stolen Unicorn	#47 The Crook Who Took the Book
#19 The Lemonade Raid	#48 The Crazy Carnival Case
#20 Hannah's Secret	#49 The Sand Castle Mystery
#21 Princess on Parade	#50 The Scarytales Sleepover
#22 The Clue in the Glue	#51 The Old-Fashioned Mystery
#23 Alien in the Classroom	#52 Big Worry in Wonderland
#24 The Hidden Treasures	#53 Recipe for Trouble
#25 Dare at the Fair	#54 The Stinky Cheese Surprise
#26 The Lucky Horseshoes	#55 The Day Camp Disaster
#27 Trouble Takes the Cake	#56 Turkey Trouble
#28 Thrill on the Hill	#57 The Carousel Mystery
#29 Lights! Camera! Clues!	#58 The Dollhouse Mystery

Available from Simon & Schuster

THE
NANCY DREW
NOTEBOOKS®

#58

The Dollhouse Mystery

CAROLYN KEENE
ILLUSTRATED BY JAN NAIMO JONES

Aladdin Paperbacks
New York   London   Toronto   Sydney

First Aladdin Paperbacks edition February 2004
Copyright © 2004 by Simon & Schuster, Inc.

ALADDIN PAPERBACKS
An imprint of Simon & Schuster
Children's Publishing Division
1230 Avenue of the Americas
New York, NY 10020

The text of this book was set in Excelsior.

Printed in the United States of America
10 9 8 7 6 5 4 3 2 1

NANCY DREW, THE NANCY DREW NOTEBOOKS, and colophon are registered trademarks of Simon & Schuster, Inc.

Library of Congress Control Number 2003113815

ISBN 0-689-86534-1

The Dollhouse Mystery

1
Baby Steps

Squirrel alert!" eight-year-old Nancy Drew said.

Nancy gripped two leashes as a little gray squirrel dashed across the sidewalk. Her puppy, Chocolate Chip, pulled at her leash. So did Baby, the other dog Nancy was walking.

"Stay, Chip!" Nancy ordered. "Stay, Baby! Stay!"

"Woof, woof, woof!" Chip barked.

"Yip, yip, yip!" Baby yapped.

Nancy grunted as she tugged both leashes. Then she shouted in her loudest voice, "Okay, you guys! Cool your jets!"

The dogs stopped barking and stared up at Nancy. As the squirrel scurried away Nancy took a deep breath. Walking two dogs wasn't easy. But she was getting good at it.

"Hi, Nancy!" a voice called.

Nancy looked up and smiled. Her best friends, Bess Marvin and George Fayne, were walking toward her.

Bess and George were cousins and in Nancy's third grade class.

Bess was dressed in white overalls and was pushing a red wheelbarrow. George was wearing blue jeans, a gray sweatshirt, and was carrying a clear plastic bag filled with cans over her shoulder.

Nancy knew why. It was the first day of Community Week—when all the kids at Carl Sandburg Elementary School helped out in the neighborhood.

"How do you like planting flowers, Bess?" Nancy asked.

Bess nodded at her wheelbarrow. It was filled with bags of soil, shovels, and packets of seeds. "Business is *blooming*!" she said with a grin. "That's a gardening joke."

Nancy giggled.

"And look at all the cans I collected for recycling!" George said. She held up her plastic bag. "I didn't know so many people liked canned peas."

Baby sniffed at a can of dog food through the bag. He belonged to Mrs. Gertrude Rutledge. Nancy's job during Community Week was to walk Baby.

The best part was that she could walk Chip along with Baby. The second best part was that Mrs. Rutledge lived in the fanciest house in River Heights!

"What kind of dog is that, Nancy?" George asked. She nodded at Baby. "He looks like a white mop without a stick."

Baby yapped at George.

"Baby is a Maltese," Nancy said. She put her finger against her lip. "And don't let Baby hear you call him a mop!"

"Are you walking Baby every day?" Bess asked.

"Just today, Wednesday, and Friday," Nancy replied. "That's when Mrs. Rutledge has tea with her granddaughters—they're twins! Mrs. Rutledge's housekeeper Olivia is too busy serving tea on those days to walk Baby."

Bess's blue eyes shone as she twirled the end of her blond ponytail.

"I heard Mrs. Rutledge's house has a swimming pool shaped like a mermaid!" Bess said. "And fountains with real goldfish!"

"And gold toilets in the bathrooms!" George added. Her dark eyes flashed. "Did you see any of that, Nancy?"

Nancy giggled. "No," she said. "But I did see something even *better*."

George ran her hand through her dark curls and asked, "What's better than a swimming pool?"

"The most beautiful old dollhouse in the whole wide world!" Nancy answered.

"A dollhouse?" Bess gasped. She gave a little jump. "I *love* dollhouses!"

"They're okay," George said with a shrug. "If you like that sort of stuff."

"Are you two sure you're cousins?" Nancy joked.

"Tell us more about the dollhouse, Nancy," Bess said. She clasped her hands together. "Pleeeease?"

Nancy shrugged her reddish-blond hair over her shoulder. "Well, Mrs. Rutledge used to play with the dollhouse when she was a little girl," she explained. "It's light purple with white trim. And the rooms have the tiniest furniture that looks so real!"

"Does it have a tiny swimming pool, too?" George asked.

"I don't know," Nancy admitted. "I only got a quick look."

"Maybe Mrs. Rutledge will let you play with it, Nancy!" Bess said excitedly.

"That would be nice," Nancy said. "But I'm there to walk Baby, not to play."

The three friends walked down the sidewalk together. Nancy let Chip and Baby stop to bark at a passing fire truck.

"I wanted to do a good job walking Baby," Nancy declared, "so I read two books all about dogs!"

"What did you find out?" George asked.

"Tons!" Nancy said. "Like the fastest dog is a greyhound. And dogs bury stuff to protect it."

Baby began chewing on the hem of George's jeans.

"Is there a chapter on ankle-biters?" George asked.

"Down, Baby!" Nancy scolded. She gave Baby's leash a gentle tug. "Down, boy!"

Baby stopped chewing.

"Wow, Nancy." Bess gasped. "You're already a great dog walker!"

Nancy hoped so. She liked walking dogs— almost as much as solving mysteries!

"I'd better bring Baby home now," Nancy decided. "It's time for his lunch."

"And when he's finished with his dog food," George said, lifting her plastic bag, "I'll take the cans!"

Nancy walked Chip and Baby back to Mrs. Rutledge's house. Olivia opened the door. She wore a black uniform with a frilly white apron.

"Would Baby like a little treat?" Olivia cooed. She dug into her apron pocket and pulled out a heart-shaped dog biscuit.

Baby yapped. He leaped up and snatched the biscuit with his teeth.

"He really likes that biscuit," Nancy said.

"Baby only eats biscuits imported from England," Olivia explained. She pulled another biscuit from her pocket. "And today Chip can have one too."

"Thank you!" Nancy said. She watched Olivia feed Chip the biscuit.

"Grrr," Baby growled. "Grrrr!"

"Oh, dear. Baby isn't used to sharing." Olivia sighed. "Why don't I take the dogs to the kitchen for some water? Baby shouldn't have a problem with that."

The dogs' paws made clicking noises on the marble floor as Olivia led them to the kitchen. Nancy followed, but as she passed the sitting room she stopped to look inside. The dollhouse was still in the middle of the room.

"Olivia?" Nancy asked. "May I please look at Mrs. Rutledge's dollhouse again?"

"Yes, but don't touch the tiny furniture," Olivia said. "I just rubbed it with a special lemon furniture oil. That furniture is very valuable!"

"It is?" Nancy asked.

Olivia nodded and said, "Mr. Vincent from the Toys of Time store wanted to buy the dollhouse furniture for lots of money."

Nancy knew Toys of Time. The toy store

was on Main Street. It sold only very old dolls, games, and toys.

"Did Mrs. Rutledge want to sell the furniture?" Nancy asked.

"No, but *I'd* like to!" Olivia muttered. "Then I could hire my *own* housekeeper!"

"Come on, dogs!" Olivia commanded as she led Chip and Baby down the hall.

Nancy slowly entered the sitting room. Besides the dollhouse there was a table set for tea and a dog bed that looked like a little human bed. It had a brass headboard and a velvet cushion with Baby's name stitched on it.

Nancy inched over to the dollhouse. It was even more beautiful up close.

She gazed inside. Miniature velvet and lace curtains hung on the windows. A doll family sat around a tiny dining room table. There was a bedroom with a canopy bed and a dresser. But Nancy's favorite was a tiny blue and white–striped sofa in the living room. The legs were shaped like animal paws!

Nancy took a whiff. Everything in the little house had a nice lemony smell!

All of a sudden Nancy heard a sound.

"Yelp! Yelp! Yelp!"

Nancy whirled around. Chip was racing into the sitting room—with something yellow tied around her tail!

"Chip!" Nancy gasped. "Who did this to you?"

2

Twin Trouble

It's okay, Chip!" Nancy said softly.

But it wasn't really okay. Someone had tied a yellow sock around Chip's tail!

Nancy quickly untied the sock. She heard a mean-sounding laugh and looked up.

A pair of twin girls stood in the room. Both had blond curly hair and wore yellow dresses. One twin looked as neat as a pin. The other one had dirt all over her face and knees—and she was wearing only one sock!

"Did you do this to my dog?" Nancy asked the grubby twin with one sock.

"Sure!" she answered with a grin. "I

wanted to see if a dog could run in circles. And she did!"

The other twin smiled sweetly at Nancy. "Hi, I'm Vicky, and this is my sister, Veronica," she said. "Are you on spring break too?"

Nancy was about to answer when Mrs. Rutledge marched in. Her silver hair was piled high on her head. Her pearl necklace glistened around her neck.

"Grandmother!" Vicky said. She pointed to Chip. "Veronica just tied her sock around that poor dog's tail."

Veronica glared at her sister.

"You have a tail too, Vicky!" she snapped. "A *tattle*-tail!"

"Veronica, wasn't the whoopie cushion on my chair this morning enough?" Mrs. Rutledge scolded. "Why can't you be nice like your sister Vicky?"

Vicky tilted her head sweetly and smiled. Veronica rolled her eyes.

I get it, Nancy thought. *Vicky is the nice twin. Veronica is the bad-news twin.*

"Is your dog hurt, Nancy?" Mrs. Rutledge asked.

"No, Mrs. Rutledge," Nancy answered. She put her arm around Chip. "Chocolate Chip seems to be okay."

"Thank goodness for that," Mrs. Rutledge said. She nodded toward the tea table. "We were just getting ready to have tea. With scones and marmalade."

"Marmalade?" Veronica said. She made a gagging sound. "I hate marmalade! I won't eat it! I won't eat it!"

"I *love* marmalade!" Vicky cooed. "Thank you, Grandmother."

Nancy had no idea what marmalade was. But she kept that to herself.

"Nancy, you must have been admiring my old dollhouse," Mrs. Rutledge said. She put her hand over her heart. "It gave me such pleasure when I was a child."

"I never saw such a beautiful dollhouse in my life!" Nancy exclaimed.

Mrs. Rutledge toyed with her string of pearls. "You did such a good job walking Baby today," she said. "Why don't you play with the dollhouse next time you come, Nancy?"

Nancy gasped. "Thank you!" *Playing with the dollhouse is a dream come true!* she thought.

"But, Grandmother," Vicky said in a soft voice. "I thought *we* were the only ones allowed to play with your dollhouse."

"We're your granddaughters," Veronica sneered. "Nancy's just a dog walker!"

Chip growled at Veronica.

"Be nice, Veronica!" Mrs. Rutledge commanded. "And if you don't wash your hands, *you* won't be allowed to play with the dollhouse!"

Veronica scowled. She wiped her dirty hands on her yellow dress.

"Hopeless!" Mrs. Rutledge sighed. She shook her head and left the room.

"Are you going to play with the dollhouse now, Nancy?" Vicky asked.

Nancy looked at her purple plastic watch. "Can't," she said. "I have to take Chip back home."

"Aw, too bad," Veronica sneered. But she didn't sound disappointed.

"I'll be back on Wednesday to walk

Baby," Nancy told Vicky. She took one last look at the dollhouse. "And to play with that awesome dollhouse!"

Nancy smiled all the way home. She couldn't wait to tell Hannah about her first day on the job.

Hannah Gruen had been the Drews' housekeeper since Nancy was three years old. She helped Mr. Drew take care of Nancy.

"That's nice of Mrs. Rutledge to let you play with her dollhouse," Hannah said when Nancy told her the news.

"She *is* nice," Nancy agreed. "So is her housekeeper Olivia. She wears a fancy uniform and serves tea in a silver teapot!"

Hannah laid a plate of cookies on the kitchen table in front of Nancy.

"Pretty fancy!" Hannah said. She pretended to show off her dress. "But *I* wear flowered dresses. And serve chocolate chip cookies on a *plastic plate*!"

Nancy leaned over and hugged Hannah around her waist. "*That's* even better!" she said with a smile.

Nancy wanted to ask Hannah what marmalade was. But her mouth was full of cookie crumbs, and then Hannah went to the living room to vacuum.

I'll ask Vicky on Wednesday, Nancy decided.

Wednesday couldn't come quickly enough for Nancy. On Tuesday morning she helped Bess plant daisies in the Drews' yard. On Tuesday afternoon she helped George collect cans on Main Street.

When Wednesday finally came Nancy jumped out of bed. She pulled on her favorite beige cargo pants and white peasant blouse. After drinking her milk and eating eggs-in-a-window, she headed straight for Mrs. Rutledge's house.

"First I'm going to walk you and Baby," Nancy told Chip on the way. "Then while you two eat those fancy dog biscuits, I'm going to play with the dollhouse."

But when Nancy reached Mrs. Rutledge's, no one looked happy to see her. Especially Mrs. Rutledge!

"What's wrong?" Nancy asked as she entered the living room. Mrs. Rutledge was pacing back and forth and holding Baby.

The twins were sitting side by side on the sofa. Olivia stood in the back near the fireplace.

"On Monday afternoon when the twins went to play with the dollhouse," Mrs. Rutledge announced, "they noticed that five pieces of furniture were missing."

Missing? Nancy stared at Mrs. Rutledge. "That's awful!" she gasped.

Nancy's mind started to race. *Does Mrs. Rutledge know I am a detective? Does she want me to find the missing furniture?* Before she could ask, Veronica pointed her finger at Nancy.

"She did it, Grandma! *Nancy* stole the dollhouse furniture!"

Nancy froze.

Had she just heard what she thought she'd heard?

3

Blamed and Framed

Y ou were playing with the dollhouse on Monday, Nancy," Veronica sneered. "So you must be the thief!"

Nancy shook her head hard. "No!" she insisted. "I did not steal the furniture!"

Chip gave a whine.

"The tiny sofa is missing," Mrs. Rutledge said. "So is the little dining-room table, the four-poster bed, the dresser, and the satin-covered chair."

Nancy remembered the tiny striped sofa. It was her favorite.

"All I did was look inside the dollhouse,"

Nancy exclaimed. "I didn't even touch the furniture!"

Mrs. Rutledge studied Nancy. She shook her head sadly. "That furniture means so much to me and is very expensive," she said.

"Very expensive!" Olivia repeated.

"So I can't take another chance," Mrs. Rutledge went on. "I'm sorry, Nancy. You can no longer play with the dollhouse, or walk Baby this week."

Nancy's heart sank. Walking Baby was her Community Week job. What would her teacher, Mrs. Reynolds, say on Monday when she found out Nancy had been fired?

"Bye, Nancy," Vicky said sweetly.

"Bye, Nancy!" Veronica sneered.

Nancy was too stunned to speak. She gave Chip's leash a tug and followed Olivia to the door. Once outside she ran to look for Bess and George in the park.

Nancy found them—hanging upside down on the monkey bars. They flipped right side up while Nancy told them everything.

"Now everyone will think I'm a dollhouse robber," Nancy said with a sigh.

"But you're not!" Bess said firmly. "You're the best detective at school!"

"That's why you have to find the *real* dollhouse robber, Nancy!" George said.

Chip sniffed at the pocket of Nancy's denim jacket. That's where she carried her blue detective notebook.

"See?" Bess laughed. "Even Chip thinks you should crack this case!"

Nancy wanted to prove that she was innocent. And finding the real dollhouse robber was the best way.

"I'll do it!" Nancy declared.

The three friends sat down on the swings. But this time they didn't swing.

Nancy pulled out her notebook and opened it to a clean page. On the top she wrote: "Who is the dollhouse robber?" Underneath she wrote the names of the furniture pieces that were missing: tiny bed, dresser, table, chair, and sofa.

"The furniture smelled lemony from Olivia's furniture polish," Nancy remembered. "And the tiny sofa had legs shaped like animal paws!"

Nancy wrote those facts in her notebook.

She tapped her chin with her pencil as she thought. "The furniture was stolen on Monday," she said. "That's when the twins were at Mrs. Rutledge's house."

"Why would they want to rob their own grandma's dollhouse?" Bess asked.

"Veronica was mad at me because I got to play with the dollhouse," Nancy answered. "Maybe she hid the furniture so she could blame it on me."

"Aha!" George declared. "Veronica is your number one suspect!"

Nancy wrote down Veronica's name. Then she wrote what she knew about her:

1) She's kind of a brat.
2) She hates marmalade.

"What's marmalade?" Bess asked.

"I think it's some kind of jelly," George said. "But I've never had it with peanut butter."

"Who else, Nancy?" Bess asked.

"Olivia the housekeeper said Mr. Vincent would pay lots of money for the tiny furniture, and if she sold it, then she wouldn't have to work for Mrs. Rutledge anymore," Nancy explained. "Mr. Vincent owns the Toys of Time store on Main Street."

"Hey! If Olivia sold him the furniture," George said, "it's probably in Toys of Time right now."

Nancy shut her notebook. "Let's go!" she said excitedly.

Main Street was two blocks away. But when Nancy, Bess, and George reached Toys of Time, Mr. Vincent blocked the door.

"Sorry," Mr. Vincent said, his mustache twitching. "Children are not allowed in this store without an adult."

"We just want to look around, Mr. Vincent," Nancy said. She didn't tell him *what* they wanted to look for.

"This is not like that store Toys 4U, where kids can go wherever they please!" Mr. Vincent scoffed. "These toys are very expensive!"

"All we want to know is if you have a dollhouse here." George sighed.

Mr. Vincent puffed out his chest. "Yes, I do!" he said. "I have an old dollhouse filled with tiny furniture!"

"Where is it?" Nancy gasped.

Mr. Vincent stepped aside so the girls could peek in. "It's right behind Freddy the Giant Teddy," he said.

Nancy could see dolls with old-fashioned dresses, armies of tin soldiers, red wagons, and a giant teddy bear.

"Thanks, Mr. Vincent!" Nancy said. They all started to walk inside. "We'll just look at the dollhouse—"

"Stop!" Mr. Vincent interrupted. He stepped in front of the girls. "I said no children allowed."

"But—," Nancy began to protest.

"Come back with your parents," Mr. Vincent said firmly. "And tell them to bring their wallets!"

Mr. Vincent slammed the door shut.

"Phooey!" Nancy said. "Now we'll never get to look at that dollhouse!"

"Out of our way! Out of our way!" a kid's voice shouted.

Nancy spun around. Six-year-olds Lonny and Lenny Wong were speeding down the block on their scooters. They were twins too. And major pests!

The girls backed up against the wall. They watched as the twins whizzed by.

"Hey!" George told Nancy. "I just thought of a way to get inside!"

"How?" Nancy asked.

George cupped her hands around her mouth. "Hey, Lonny! Lenny!" she yelled. "Mr. Vincent is giving away free Panda Bars inside his store!"

Nancy watched the twins screech to a stop. She knew they loved Panda ice-cream bars more than anything!

"Panda Bars?" Lenny shouted.

"All right!" Lonny cheered.

George held the door open as the twins scooted inside. Nancy could see Mr. Vincent chasing them around the store!

"Inside!" Nancy whispered.

In a flash the girls sneaked into the store and hid behind the giant teddy bear.

"There *is* a dollhouse back here!" Bess whispered. She stared at the old dollhouse set on a pedestal. But the rooms were facing the wall.

"We have to turn the dollhouse all the way around," Nancy whispered.

The girls each grabbed a corner of the dollhouse. They grunted as they turned it around on the pedestal.

Nancy looked inside the dollhouse. The rooms *were* filled with old-fashioned tiny furniture.

"Do you see Mrs. Rutledge's missing furniture?" George asked softly.

"I'm not sure," Nancy whispered. "I have to stand back and get a better look."

But as Nancy stepped back, she bumped into the giant teddy bear.

"HELLO!" a voice cried out. "I'M FREDDY! YOUR VERY OWN TEDDY!"

Nancy froze. *What was that?*

"Nancy!" George hissed. "You flipped a switch that made the bear talk!"

"HELLO! I'M FREDDY—"

"Oh no!" Nancy whispered. "Now Mr. Vincent will know we're back here!"

The girls searched everywhere for another switch. But it was too late!

"Aha!" Mr. Vincent shouted as he peeked behind Freddy. "Thought you could sneak past me, hmmm?"

4

Bow-Wow Bandit

We *had* to check out your dollhouse, Mr. Vincent!" Nancy declared.

"HELLO, I'M FREDDY—"

"Put a sock in it!" Mr. Vincent told the teddy bear. He gave the bear's ear three tugs. It stopped talking!

"So that's how it works," George said, smiling. "Your store *is* neat. Even if most of the stuff is pretty old."

"Now!" Mr. Vincent said. "Why did you have to see the dollhouse?"

Nancy told Mr. Vincent all about the missing furniture. And about Olivia.

"I wanted to buy Mrs. Rutledge's dollhouse furniture for years," Mr. Vincent admitted. "But she would never sell it to me. And Olivia never tried! You can see for yourself," Mr. Vincent said. He pointed to the dollhouse. "Do you *see* any of the missing furniture in there?"

Nancy stared at the dollhouse. The only missing piece she remembered seeing was the tiny striped sofa. How would she know if the other pieces were there? Unless . . .

"Mr. Vincent," Nancy said. "If you don't mind, I'd like to perform a test."

Mr. Vincent's mustache twitched again. "What kind of test?" he asked.

"A sniff test!" Nancy replied. "Olivia rubs the tiny furniture with lemon oil. So the missing pieces would smell nice and lemony."

Mr. Vincent raised an eyebrow. "What are you?" he asked. "Some kid-detective?"

"The best!" Bess said with a smile. "She's Nancy Drew!"

Nancy stepped closer to the dollhouse. She took one long whiff.

"Not lemony at all," Nancy declared. "In fact, it smells more like Flakey Wakey cereal!"

Mr. Vincent cleared his throat.

George turned to Mr. Vincent. "Did you get your furniture from a *cereal box*?"

Mr. Vincent started to blush. "Do you know how much cereal I had to eat just to fill that dollhouse?" he asked.

"It's okay, Mr. Vincent," Nancy said, smiling. "Your secret is safe with us."

Mr. Vincent waved the girls out from behind the teddy bear. Then he disappeared behind a pile of game boxes. He came out a few seconds later wearing a pair of weird-looking glasses!

"Surprise!" Mr. Vincent announced.

The girls stared at the glasses. The lenses made Mr. Vincent's eyes look HUGE!

"What are those?" George asked.

"They're Detective Danny Magnifying Glasses!" Mr. Vincent explained. "And I'll sell them to you for just a nickel."

"A nickel?" Nancy asked. "They've got to be more expensive than a nickel!"

"Okay—a penny!" Mr. Vincent said, smiling. "But that's my final offer."

Nancy smiled. She pulled out a penny and gave it to Mr. Vincent. He then handed her the Detective Danny glasses.

"Thanks!" Nancy said. She looked through the goofy-looking glasses. Everything around her seemed gigantic!

"Enjoy the glasses, Detective Drew, and next time come with a grown-up," Mr. Vincent said as he led Nancy, Bess, and George to the door.

The girls left the Toys of Time store and stood on Main Street.

"Olivia is no longer a suspect," Nancy said. She crossed Olivia out of her notebook. "Now it's just Veronica!"

"I'll bet my soccer jersey that she hid the furniture," George insisted.

"But we have no evidence against Veronica yet!" Nancy admitted.

"How's this for evidence?" George asked. "She's a BRAT!"

"Come on, George," Bess said. "We need to work on our Community Week jobs."

Nancy said good-bye to Bess and George. Nancy wanted to go home to talk to her father about the missing dollhouse furniture.

Mr. Drew was a lawyer. He helped Nancy with her homework and with most of her detective cases.

"Hi, Daddy!" Nancy said when she got home. She walked into the den wearing the Detective Danny glasses. "What big ears you've got!"

"Big ears?" Mr. Drew looked up from his newspaper. Then he laughed. "Hey! I had a pair of Detective Danny glasses when I was a kid. Where did you get those?"

"At Toys of Time," Nancy answered. "Mr. Vincent sold them to me for only a penny. Why do you think he did that?"

"Mr. Vincent knows that old toys are special," Mr. Drew said, "and that they should be shared."

"Just like Mrs. Rutledge shared her dollhouse with me." Nancy sighed. She told her Dad all about the dollhouse and the missing furniture.

"Would you like me to talk to Mrs.

Rutledge, Pudding Pie?" Mr. Drew asked.

Nancy knew it would help. But she never started a case she didn't finish.

"I'm going to do everything I can to catch the real dollhouse robber!" Nancy said. She put the glasses back on. "Even if I have to wear *these* goofy things!"

"Let's question Veronica today!" Bess said the next day. She was pushing her wheelbarrow filled with garden tools. The girls were looking for more people to help for Community Week.

George lugged her bag filled with cans over her shoulder. "Maybe there's a Detective Danny lie-detector kit," she said. "Then we could use it on Veronica!"

Nancy shook her head. "It's Thursday," she replied. "Veronica and Vicky aren't visiting today."

They walked up Crescent Street toward Mrs. Rutledge's house.

"I really miss walking Baby." Nancy sighed. She gazed at the big white house. "I wonder what he's up to."

A tiny dog door on the side of the house

sprang open. Baby leaped out. He ran around the house toward the backyard.

"It's Baby!" Nancy exclaimed.

"Look at him go!" Bess said.

"It looked like he had something in his mouth," George said. "Where's he going?"

Bess parked her wheelbarrow next to a tree. George dropped her bag of cans next to it. Then the three girls raced around the house. They looked over a fence into the backyard.

"Look," Bess whispered. "Baby is burying something."

Nancy watched Baby dig. There were four other little hills of fresh dirt in the yard.

"Baby already buried four other things," Nancy whispered.

"So?" George asked.

"So do the math," Nancy whispered. "There were five pieces of missing furniture!"

Bess and George stared at the yard. Then they stared at Nancy with wide eyes.

"Ohmigosh!" Bess squealed. "Could the dollhouse robber be Baby?"

5

Hide and Sneak

"Baby is just being a dog," Nancy said. "Whatever he buried, he buried to protect it. Just like the book said."

"But why would Baby want to protect tiny dollhouse furniture?" Bess asked.

"I don't know," Nancy admitted. "But first we have to dig up those hills to see what's underneath."

When Baby finished burying he looked up. He scurried over to Nancy and wagged his tail. "Yap, yap, yap!" he barked.

"Not so loud, Baby," Nancy murmured. She petted him through the fence. "I'm not allowed to be with you anymore."

Baby looked sad as the girls walked away from the Rutledge house.

"If you're not allowed to be here, Nancy," Bess said, "how are we going to dig in the backyard?"

"I know! We could climb over the fence and dig really fast," George said excitedly. "I'm good at climbing!"

Nancy shook her head. "If Mrs. Rutledge or Olivia catch us sneaking into the backyard, we'll all be in trouble."

"I have a better idea!" Bess told Nancy. "Maybe I can plant flowers in Mrs. Rutledge's backyard. And you can hide in my wheelbarrow!"

"Hide in the wheelbarrow?" Nancy repeated slowly.

Bess nodded. "I can wheel you into the backyard. Then you can jump out and start digging!" she said.

"But what if Mrs. Rutledge sees me back there?" Nancy asked. "Or Olivia?"

"I can keep them busy by collecting cans," George offered.

Nancy thought about it. Hiding in the wheelbarrow seemed a little weird. But it was the only way to get into the backyard!

"Let's do it," Nancy declared.

Bess yanked everything out of the wheelbarrow and piled it behind a tree. Then Nancy climbed in and covered herself with a dark green blanket.

"This blanket is dusty!" Nancy said, coughing. "What do you use it for, Bess?"

"I kneel on it when I plant flowers," Bess said. "You don't expect me to get my new gardening overalls dirty, do you?"

"Give me a break!" George groaned.

Nancy held on as the wheelbarrow tipped. She could feel Bess pushing it over the bumpy path to Mrs. Rutledge's door.

Just then it jerked to a stop.

From under the blanket Nancy could hear George ringing the doorbell. After a few rings she heard the door squeak open.

"Yes?" Olivia's voice asked.

"Hello," George said. "My cousin Bess and I are doing community work for our school. I'd like to collect your cans."

"And I'd like to plant flowers in your yard," Bess added. "Your *back*yard. In about five places!"

Nancy groaned to herself. Too much information!

"Sorry, girls," Olivia said, "but Mrs. Rutledge has a gardener. And I do the recycling in the house."

"Wait!" George called. "You would be helping us with our Community Week jobs."

"Why, what a wonderful idea!" another voice piped up.

It's Mrs. Rutledge! Nancy thought.

"I wish my granddaughter Veronica would do Community Week." Mrs. Rutledge sighed. "It would keep her out of mischief."

Then Nancy heard Mrs. Rutledge say, "Olivia, let these girls do their jobs!"

"Yes, ma'am," Olivia said. She led George into the kitchen to collect cans.

Nancy felt Bess push the wheelbarrow all the way to the backyard. It was a bumpy ride. When it finally stopped, Bess whispered, "The coast is clear, Nancy. You can hop out now!"

Nancy was glad to throw off the dusty blanket and climb out of the wheelbarrow.

"Let's start digging," Nancy said.

"With what?" Bess gasped. "I left my tools behind the tree!"

"Then we'll use our hands!" Nancy said. She shaped hers to look like paws. "If they're good enough for Baby, they're good enough for us!"

"Woof, woof!" Bess joked.

Nancy ran to one hill on the ground. Bess ran to another. Then the two started digging quickly with their hands.

Nancy dug and dug. Then her hand hit something. Something tiny and hard!

"Bess!" Nancy hissed. "I think I found something!"

6

Chew and Clue

What is it, Nancy?" Bess asked. "Is it the tiny sofa? Or the little table?"

Nancy brushed aside the dirt. She looked down at the ground and groaned.

"It's a *dog biscuit*!"

"A what?" Bess cried.

Nancy picked up the heart-shaped biscuit. "Baby buried his imported English dog biscuit!" she said.

Nancy and Bess dug up four more dog biscuits. When they were done they sat on the ground.

"I wonder why Baby would want to protect his dog biscuits," Bess said.

Nancy wondered too. Until she remembered the book she had read about dogs.

"Baby didn't like *Chip* eating his biscuits," Nancy said, "so he probably buried them to keep them from her."

Bess breathed a sigh of relief. "So Baby *was* just being a dog," she said. "And not a dollhouse robber."

Nancy was about to stand up when she heard a voice from inside.

"Yoo-hoo!" Mrs. Rutledge called out. "How about some nice cold lemonade, young lady?"

"Wait, Mrs. Rutledge!" George's voice was saying. "Don't go back there. Please. I need more help with the cans!"

Nancy stared at Bess. "Mrs. Rutledge is coming!" she hissed.

"Quick!" Bess whispered back. "Get back in the wheelbarrow!"

Nancy scooped dirt over the biscuits. Then she climbed inside the wheelbarrow and covered herself with the blanket.

Nancy held her breath and heard Bess say, "H-h-hello, Mrs. Rutledge!"

"Hello, dear," Mrs. Rutledge said. "Here's Olivia with the lemonade."

"I hope *you* like my lemonade," Olivia said. "Veronica says it tastes like swamp water."

"Oh, that Veronica!" Mrs. Rutledge scoffed. "But *Vicky* loves lemonade!"

Nancy felt the wheelbarrow shake just a bit. Then she heard a snuffling noise.

Uh-oh—it's Baby! Nancy thought. *He knows I'm in here!*

"Grrrph," Baby snuffled. "Grrph!"

"Baby seems interested in that wheelbarrow," Mrs. Rutledge said. "What kind of seeds do you have in there?"

"Um," Bess started to say. "Er—"

"Dogwood!" George blurted. "What dog doesn't like dogwood trees?"

Nancy held her breath. Baby was jumping against the wheelbarrow hard!

"Something isn't right," Mrs. Rutledge said. "Why don't I look inside the wheelbarrow?"

Oh, no! Nancy thought. *When Mrs. Rutledge finds me in here, I'll be toast!*

"We have to go now!" George blurted.

"Right away!" Bess agreed.

45

"But what about the flowers you were supposed to plant?" Mrs. Rutledge asked.

"It looks like you didn't do anything."

"I just found out I'm allergic to flowers!" Bess said quickly. "Ah-chooo!"

"Thanks, Mrs. Rutledge," George said. "We'll take a raincheck on that lemonade!"

The wheelbarrow jerked. Nancy could feel herself being wheeled away—fast!

"Wait!" Olivia's voice called out. "You forgot your cans!"

Nancy held on until the wheelbarrow stopped bumping. Then she heard Bess say, "We're on the sidewalk, Nancy. You can come out now!"

The dusty blanket fell off as Nancy straightened up. She felt woozy as she climbed out.

"All that for a bunch of dog biscuits," Nancy groaned.

"And we didn't even get to drink that lemonade." Bess sighed.

The girls found the pile of gardening tools Bess had left behind a tree. They reloaded the wheelbarrow.

"What should we do next?" Bess asked.

"Let's head to the Double Dip," Nancy said. Her head was still spinning from the bumpy ride. "I need an ice-cream break!"

The girls walked to their favorite ice-cream parlor on Main Street. On the way they saw lots of kids from school working on their Community Week projects.

"How do you like our masterpiece?" Kyle Leddington called. He and Peter DeSands were painting benches dark green.

Mari Cheng was delivering groceries on her bike. Even Jason Hutchings, David Berger, and Mike Minelli had a job. They were scraping gum off the sidewalk.

"It's a yucky job!" Jason bragged. He pretended to flex his arm muscle. "But somebody's got to do it!"

"Yeah!" George called. "Especially since most of the gum was *yours*!"

Nancy giggled. The boys were the biggest troublemakers in her class.

Then Nancy saw their friend Katie Zaleski walking toward them. She had a strawberry ice-cream cone in one hand, and her pet parrot Lester was sitting on her shoulder.

"Hi, guys!" Katie called. She didn't notice Lester pecking at her ice cream.

"Hi, Katie!" Nancy said. "What kind of Community Week job do you have?"

"I just started walking this dog named Baby," Katie said.

"That used to be my job," Nancy said.

"I wish it still was," Katie groaned. "I've been walking Baby since Wednesday and I hate it!"

"Why?" Nancy asked.

"Baby yaps all the time," Katie replied. "And Mrs. Rutledge's granddaughter Veronica taught Lester a bad word."

"Doodlehead! Doodlehead! Arrrk!" Lester squawked.

"See?" Katie asked. "And Baby chews on furniture, too."

"He does?" Nancy asked. She couldn't remember seeing Baby chew on Mrs. Rutledge's furniture.

"I'll show you," Katie said. "I have the sofa in my pocket."

"How can you have a sofa in your pocket?" Bess laughed.

Katie dug into her jacket pocket and said, "Because it's a teeny-tiny sofa!"

Nancy stared at Katie.

"Did you say 'teeny-tiny sofa'?"

7

In a Jam

"Check it out," Katie said. She pulled a tiny striped sofa from her pocket and held it up. "I saw Baby chewing on it when I walked him on Wednesday. It looks like it's from some kind of dollhouse."

Nancy stared at the sofa. It had the same blue and white stripes as the missing sofa. And legs shaped like animal paws!

"It's the missing sofa," Nancy exclaimed. "I know it is!"

Katie looked confused. "Can someone tell me what's going on?" she asked.

Nancy told Katie everything. She told her about the missing furniture and about how

Veronica accused Nancy of stealing it.

"I wonder if the tiny sofa smells lemony," Bess said.

"It probably smells like dog breath!" Katie groaned. "I didn't want Baby to swallow it so I put it in my pocket. But I forgot to give it back to Mrs. Rutledge."

Nancy held out her hand. "Can you lend me the sofa for a day, Katie? I need it as evidence," she said.

"Sure." Katie handed Nancy the tiny sofa. "But take real good care of it. Or else I'll lose my job too!"

"You already lost your ice cream!" Bess giggled. She pointed to Katie's half-eaten ice-cream cone.

"What?" Katie cried. She looked at her ice-cream cone, then at Lester. "Bad parrot! Bad parrot!"

"Doodlehead!" Lester squawked. "Doodlehead! Arrrk!"

Katie rolled her eyes. "I'd better have a talk with Lester," she said. "See you later!"

After Katie walked away, Nancy jumped up and down. "Yippee!" she cheered. "Baby found one of the missing pieces!"

"But where was it?" Bess asked.

Nancy studied the tiny sofa. It didn't have dirt or grass stains on it.

"Whoever stole the sofa probably hid it inside the house," Nancy decided. "So the four other pieces must be there too."

"Let's examine the little sofa real close," George suggested. "Maybe we can find some more clues."

The three girls ran to a nearby bench. They sat down side by side.

"Okay," Nancy said. She held up the striped sofa. "What do you see?"

"A tiny sofa!" Bess said, smiling.

"No duh!" George groaned.

Nancy examined the sofa for evidence. But it was too tiny. "I wish I had my magnifying glass," she said.

Then Nancy remembered the Detective Danny glasses. They were folded inside her back pocket!

"I knew these would come in handy one of these days," Nancy said, pulling out the glasses. She put them on and studied the sofa. It didn't look so tiny anymore!

"I see teeth marks," Nancy said. "Probably from Baby."

"Or Veronica!" George joked.

Nancy looked closer. She saw a stain on the cushion. An orange stain.

"I wonder where that orange stain came from," Nancy said.

She opened her notebook and wrote down all of the orange things they could think of: orange juice, sweet potatoes, carrots, and tangerines.

"Baby wouldn't eat any of that stuff," Nancy pointed out.

"So whoever took the tiny sofa took it with messy hands," Bess decided.

Nancy looked up. The word "messy" made her think of one person—Veronica!

"Mrs. Rutledge said that Veronica's hands are always messy," Nancy said. "I even saw her wipe them on her dress!"

"That *is* messy!" Bess cried.

"Maybe Veronica had orange stuff all over her hands when she took the sofa!" George pointed out.

Nancy held the sofa carefully. She still wasn't sure how the stain had gotten there.

But she was going to find out!

"We have to go to Mrs. Rutledge's house tomorrow to talk to Veronica," Nancy decided, "face-to-face!"

Just then Kyle Leddington walked over. He was carrying a cardboard sign under his arm.

"Hi, Kyle," Nancy said, smiling. "What's that?"

Kyle didn't smile back. "It's . . . a sign," he said. "I forgot to hang it up."

"What does it say?" Bess asked.

Kyle flipped the sign over. It read WET PAINT!

"Eeeek!" the girls shrieked. They jumped up and whirled around. Their backs were covered with dark green paint!

"Yuck!" Nancy cried.

"S-sorry!" Kyle stammered. Then he turned and ran away.

"Oh no!" Bess groaned. "My brand-new spring pants are ruined."

"Now we found four stains!" George chuckled. "One on the tiny sofa—and three on us!"

Nancy forced herself to smile.

"Yeah," she said. "But at least one of the stains was a *clue*!"

"What if Veronica won't talk to you, Nancy?" Bess asked the next day.

Nancy rang Mrs. Rutledge's doorbell. Her detective notebook and the tiny sofa were in her pink waistpack. "She will when I show her the tiny sofa," she said. "And the messy stain!"

Olivia opened the door. She was rubbing one of her eyes with her fist.

"What happened, Olivia?" Nancy asked.

"That Veronica!" Olivia spat. "I was serving tea, and she squirted me in the eye with a lemon!"

Nancy smiled to herself. At least Veronica was in the house!

"May we speak to Veronica, please?" Nancy asked. "It's very important."

Olivia blinked her sore eye. "You aren't allowed to come back," she said. "But maybe you can keep Veronica busy and out of trouble for a few minutes!"

Olivia stepped away from the door. "Come in and wait in the sitting room," she said. "And I'll get Miss Veronica."

The girls filed into Mrs. Rutledge's house. Bess and George looked around.

"Wow!" Bess gasped. "This house is a mansion. Just like in the movies!"

"I'll bet it *does* have gold toilet seats!" George exclaimed.

Nancy led Bess and George to the sitting room.

"There's the dollhouse!" Bess gasped. She ran to it. "It's beeeeeautiful!"

Nancy looked at the tea table. There was a plate of yummy-looking scones and a small jar of jam. Nancy read the label on the jar: KINGSLEY'S ORANGE MARMALADE.

Orange Marmalade?

So that's what marmalade was. It was orange jam!

I wonder if the orange stain came from marmalade, Nancy thought. She pulled the tiny sofa from her waistpack. But before she could match the stain—

"Hey, Nancy!" George called. "Check it out!"

Nancy spun around. George was sitting on Baby's brass dog bed!

"George, get off," Nancy scolded. "That's Baby's bed!"

"You mean that little dog has such a fancy bed?" Bess asked.

George stood up. "Fancy-shmancy!" she said. "That bed is totally lumpy."

"Lumpy?" Nancy asked. She handed Bess the tiny sofa. Then she knelt by the bed and ran her hand over the velvety cushion.

"It *does* feel lumpy," Nancy said.

"That's weird," Bess said. "Mrs. Rutledge wouldn't let her precious Baby sleep on a lumpy bed."

Nancy stared at the dog bed. "Unless," she said slowly, "there's something underneath that's making it lumpy!"

8

Ready, Set, Play!

Quickly Nancy lifted the cushion and gasped. Underneath was a tiny table, bed, dresser, and chair!

"Ohmigosh!" Nancy cried. "It's the rest of the missing furniture!"

"What are you doing?" a voice snapped.

Nancy jumped up and whirled around. Veronica was standing at the door. Nancy knew it was Veronica because her knees were dirty.

"You're not allowed in here!" Veronica sneered. "You're the dollhouse robber!"

"Olivia let us in fair and square, Veronica," Nancy said. She stepped away from the dog bed. "And it's a good thing she did, because look what we found!"

Veronica looked at the tiny furniture. Her mouth dropped wide open.

"How did *that* get there?" she asked.

Bess held up the tiny sofa. "Why don't *you* tell *us*, Veronica?" she asked.

Nancy scooped up all of the furniture. It all had orange stains.

"I didn't hide the furniture!" Veronica insisted. "You're nuts!"

Then she ran out of the room.

"Stop her!" George shouted.

The girls dropped all of the tiny furniture on Baby's bed. They raced out of the room and chased Veronica down a long hallway.

Veronica reached the end of the hall and skidded around a corner. Nancy and her friends were about to do the same until Vicky popped out of a doorway—SLAM!

Nancy bumped right into Vicky. She felt something crunch against her chest.

Something wet and sticky!

Nancy looked down. Her shirt had a big orange stain on it. So did Vicky's.

"Yuck!" Nancy said.

"My fault,"Vicky said. She scraped a piece of crushed toast from her shirt. "I shouldn't eat and walk at the same time."

"And I shouldn't run in the house," Nancy admitted. She stared at the bright orange stain on Vicky's shirt. It was the exact same color as the sofa stain!

"Is that marmalade?" Nancy asked.

Vicky smiled and nodded. "Veronica doesn't eat marmalade," she said. "So I get to eat all of it. Am I lucky or what?"

Vicky gave a little wave. Then she walked up the hall and turned the corner.

Nancy turned to Bess and George.

"The stains on the furniture were orange marmalade!" she said excitedly.

"So?" George asked.

"Veronica never eats marmalade," Nancy said, "but Vicky does!"

"Nancy!" Bess gasped. "Are you saying the stains came from Vicky's hands?"

"Vicky's so nice," George said. "Why would she hide the dollhouse furniture?"

Nancy wasn't sure. Until she saw a box of dog biscuits next to Baby's bed.

"Baby hid his biscuits so Chip couldn't

eat them," Nancy said. "Maybe Vicky hid the furniture so I couldn't play with it."

Nancy called to Vicky. She came into the sitting room wearing a clean blouse. But when Vicky saw the tiny furniture on Baby's bed her mouth dropped open.

"Y-y-you found it!" Vicky stammered. She looked scared.

"Vicky?" Nancy asked. "All of the missing furniture pieces had orange stains on them. And you love orange marmalade."

Vicky stared at Nancy. "I didn't hide the furniture!" she said. "I didn't!"

"There's Nancy, Grandma!" Veronica's voice shouted. "The dollhouse robber!"

Nancy spun around. Veronica was storming into the room with Mrs. Rutledge. Olivia was right behind them.

"Nancy!" Mrs. Rutledge said with a frosty voice. "You weren't supposed to come back here."

"Maybe she came back to steal more furniture, Grandma!" Veronica sneered. She pointed to Bess and George. "And this time she brought help!"

Nancy stepped up to Mrs. Rutledge.

"Bess and George are helping me *find* the missing furniture, Mrs. Rutledge," she said. "Not steal it!"

"Nancy's a detective," George declared. "And look what she found!"

"Ta-daa!" Bess sang. She waved her hand toward Baby's bed and the furniture.

"The furniture!" Olivia gasped.

"Oh, my!" Mrs. Rutledge said. "Where did you find it?"

"Under Baby's bed," George explained. "And it all has marmalade stains on it, too!"

"Marmalade?" Mrs. Rutledge asked. She seemed to think about it. Then she turned to Vicky. "Don't tell me *you* took the missing furniture, Victoria!"

"Vicky?" Veronica stared at her twin. "Miss Goody-good? How come?"

Vicky's eyes darted back and forth from her grandmother to Veronica. Her shoulders dropped and she sighed.

"I didn't want Nancy to play with the dollhouse," Vicky confessed. "So on Monday I hid some furniture under Baby's bed.

I was right! Nancy thought.

"I didn't want Nancy to be blamed,"

Vicky went on. "I just wanted to keep my favorite pieces to myself. Like the bed, the sofa, and the little chair!"

"Vicky, I'm shocked!" Mrs. Rutledge exclaimed.

"Because I took the dollhouse furniture?" Vicky asked softly.

"Yes!" Mrs. Rutledge said. "And because you had marmalade on your hands. You're usually so neat!"

"It's about time!" Veronica cheered. She began jumping up and down. "For once I'm not the sloppy one. And for once I'm not in trouble. Woo-hoo!"

Nancy smiled. She had solved the case and proved she was innocent, too!

"Sorry, Nancy," Vicky said. Then she turned to Mrs. Rutledge. "Sorry, Grandma. You probably don't like me very much now."

"Nonsense!" Mrs. Rutledge said. "I'm just a little disappointed in you, Victoria."

Mrs. Rutledge walked over to the dollhouse. She placed her hand on it lovingly.

"When I was a little girl I shared my dollhouse with *all* my friends," Mrs. Rutledge said. "What good is having something special if you can't share it?"

"Wow, Mrs. Rutledge," Nancy said. "That's exactly what my dad said."

"Then your dad is a very wise man," Mrs. Rutledge said with a smile.

Veronica turned to Nancy. "Are you really a detective?" she asked.

"Yes," Nancy said, "but I have lots of help. From Bess and George—"

"And Detective Danny!" Bess cut in with a smile.

Vicky smiled too. "I have an idea!" she said. "Let's *all* play with the dollhouse. Together!"

"Goody gumdrops!" Bess said, jumping up and down.

"I'll just watch." George sighed. "I'm not really into dollhouses."

Veronica looked at George with surprise. "Me neither!" she said. "Do you want to kick a soccer ball in the yard?"

"Cool!" George exclaimed. She and Veronica high-fived.

Nancy smiled as the two ran out of the sitting room. Maybe Veronica wasn't as bad as she seemed!

"And how about you, Nancy?" Mrs. Rutledge asked. "Would you like to play with my dollhouse?"

Just then, the doorbell rang. Olivia opened the door and Katie stepped inside.

"I'm here to walk Baby," she said, but she didn't look very excited about it.

Nancy had an idea. She gave Mrs. Rutledge her biggest smile. "Maybe I'll play with the dollhouse later, Mrs. Rutledge. If Katie doesn't mind, I'd like to walk Baby again!"

"You would?" Katie asked, a grin spreading across her face, "I mean, sure you can walk him, Nancy—if it's ok with you, Mrs. Rutledge."

"It's just fine with me, girls," Mrs. Rutledge said with a smile.

Baby ran into the room. He jumped into Nancy's arms and licked her face.

"It's the last day of Community Week," Nancy said, "and I have a job to do."

Nancy and Baby stepped outside with Katie.

"I'm glad we solved the case of the disappearing dollhouse furniture," Nancy said. "I'm also really happy to have my job back!"

"I'm happy you got your job back too . . . nothing personal, Baby!" Katie said with a wave good-bye to Nancy.

Nancy waved back and then walked Baby up and down the streets of River Heights.

But that night while Nancy was up in her room she had one more job to do.

She kicked off her sneakers, sat on her bed, and opened up her detective notebook. Then she began to write. . . .

Community Week was a HUGE success! I got to walk Baby AND solve a case— all in one spring break.

I'm happy that Mrs. Rutledge has a whole dollhouse back again. I guess Daddy was right when he said old toys are very, very special. Just like old—and new—friends!

Case closed!

She's sharp.

She's smart.

She's confident.

She's unstoppable.

And she's on your trail.

MEET THE NEW NANCY DREW

Still sleuthing,

still solving crimes,

ut she's got some new tricks up her sleeve!

NANCY DREW

girl detective

MARGARET PETERSON HADDIX

the GIRL with 500 middle NAMES

JANIE WHO?

It's hard enough being the **new** kid in school. It's even **tougher** when all of your new classmates live in big houses and wear expensive **clothes**, while your parents have little and are risking everything just to give you a chance at a better life.

Now Janie's about to do something that will make her stand out even more among the rich **kids** at Satterthwaite School. Something that will have everyone **wondering** just who Janie Sams really is. And something that will mean totally unexpected changes for Janie and her **family**.

ALADDIN PAPERBACKS
Simon & Schuster Children's Publishing • www.SimonSaysKids.com

THIRD-GRADE DETECTIVES

Everyone in the third grade loves the new teacher, Mr. Merlin.

Mr. Merlin used to be a spy, and he knows all about secret codes and the strange and gross ways the police solve mysteries.

YOU CAN HELP DECODE THE CLUES AND SOLVE THE MYSTERY IN THESE OTHER STORIES ABOUT THE THIRD-GRADE DETECTIVES:

#1 The Clue of the Left-handed Envelope

#2 The Puzzle of the Pretty Pink Handkerchief

#3 The Mystery of the Hairy Tomatoes

#4 The Cobweb Confession

#5 The Riddle of the Stolen Sand

#6 The Secret of the Green Skin

#7 The Case of the Dirty Clue

#8 The Secret of the Wooden Witness

Coming Soon: #9 The Case of the Sweaty Bank Robber

DDIN PAPERBACKS • Simon & Schuster Children's Publishing • www.SimonSaysKids.com

Ready-for-Chapters

HITTY'S TRAVELS #1: Civil War Days

Hitty's owner, Nell, lives on a plantation in North Carolina. When a house slave named Sarina comes to work for Nell's father, the girls become friends. But when Nell and Sarina break the rules of the plantation, things will never be the same again. . . .

HITTY'S TRAVELS #2: Gold Rush Days

Hitty's owner, Annie, is excited to travel with her father to California in search of gold, but it's a tough journey out West and an even tougher life when they arrive. Annie longs to help out, but is there anything she can do?

HITTY'S TRAVELS #3: Voting Rights Days

Hitty's owner, Emily, lives in Washington, D.C. Emily's aunt Ada and many other women are trying to win the right to vote. But when the women are put in jail, all hope seems lost. Will Emily—and Hitty—find a way to help the cause?

HITTY'S TRAVELS #4: Ellis Island Days

Hitty travels to Italy in style with a spoiled little rich girl, but soon falls into the hands of Fiorella Rossi, a kind girl whose poor family longs to reach America. Will the Rossis survive the awful conditions of their long journey?

Available from Aladdin Paperbacks
Published by Simon & Schuster